SLOW RIDE

LORELEI JAMES

Slow Ride

by Lorelei James

A Rough Riders Novella, Book 9.5

Ridgeview Publishing

ISBN: 978-1-941869-21-5

Visit www.loreleijames.com

Cover Design by Meredith Blair
Cover Image © GM photo/Bigstock.com/24636797
Edited by Lindsey Faber
Interior Design by BB eBooks Co., Ltd. – www.bbebooksthailand.com

Author's New Note: I wrote *Slow Ride* in 2010 as a gift to my readers for sticking with me through 9 full-length Rough Riders books. While my existing readers were happy to revisit Jack and Keely, anyone unfamiliar with the Rough Riders world that downloaded the free edition of this digital-only short story were confused because *Slow Ride* is not exactly a standalone story—the Rough Riders completed saga of 16 novels and 4 short story/novellas are meant to be read in chronological order.

Now that the publishing rights have reverted to me, I've opted to keep *Slow Ride* as its own installment in the series. I've added the epilogue from *All Jacked Up*, which is a lead in to *Slow Ride*, as well as a peek a few years down the road when Jack and Keely start their family in *All Knocked Up* from the *Short Rides* anthology.

Enjoy!
~Lorelei, 2017

Timeline: *Slow Ride* takes place between the epilogue of Rough Riders book 8, *All Jacked Up*, and the second chapter of Rough Riders book 10, *Cowgirls Don't Cry*.

Epilogue from

ALL JACKED UP

KEELY SUSPECTED SHE resembled a ghost more than a bride. She leaned closer to the lighted mirror and scrutinized her reflection. Scratch that. Maybe the *Bride of Frankenstein*. Yikes. Why had they gobbed so much gunk on her face? Especially when her face was completely covered? She batted at the frothy white veil, knocking the headpiece off-center. Again.

"Stop fidgeting," Chassie hissed, smoothing the gossamer fabric back in place.

The door to the bedroom opened. Women scurried forward in case Jack might try to sneak in.

Keely smiled, hoping he *would* attempt to infiltrate the inner sanctum and cart her off.

But a collective sigh echoed as the minister waltzed in and asked, "Has anyone seen the ring bearer?"

"Which one? I have six." Keely had drafted her oldest nephews for the wedding party. They'd drawn straws to decide which unlucky sucker got stuck carrying the "girly" satin pillow.

"I'm looking for the ring bearer with the rings."

"Gib is missing?"

No one answered. Maybe because no one had heard her over the din of giggles and gossip?

Seizing the opportunity to escape, Keely muttered, "I'll find him." She tried to stand; her butt was firmly shoved back down on the tufted velvet chair.

"Nice try, missy, but park it. You're not going anywhere." India jammed more pearl-coated bobby pins in her hair.

"Ouch!"

"Oh, don't be such a baby. You didn't whine this much when I tattooed you."

"Stop gnawing on your lip too, or you'll smudge your gloss," Domini added as she shifted Markus on her hip, directing his grabbing hands away from the veil.

Just wait until the minister pronounced them husband and wife. Keely planned to smear the carefully applied gloss all over Jack's lips. Then she'd rip off the ridiculous headpiece and stomp on it with the equally ridiculous pointy-toed satin shoes.

Temper temper.

Love aside, why did people go through this rigmarole? No wonder couples eloped. She and Jack could've skipped this part and gotten straight to the good stuff: the island honeymoon.

She blew out a frustrated breath, twisting away from the array of beauty products, which ensured she didn't look one bit like herself on the biggest day of her life. Would Jack even recognize her?

A tiny hand tugged on her sequined sleeve. Keely sucked in a surprised breath at the unyielding fit of the wedding gown when she bent at the waist. "Yes, Eliza," she said, squinting at the beribboned flower girl through the gauzy veil.

"I know where Gib is."

At least someone was worried about the missing ring bearer. "Where?"

"He threw up in the bathroom 'bout five minutes ago."

"What?" Panic escalated along with her voice. "Is he sick?"

A sneer wrinkled Eliza's pert nose. "He's not sick, he's stupid. Kyler dared him to drink—" Her eyes widened, she clapped a gloved hand over her mouth and started to back away.

But not fast enough. Keely grabbed her spindly arm. "What did Gib drink?"

"Pickle juice," Eliza blurted.

"Pickle juice?" Keely repeated. "Where on earth did he find pickle juice?"

Eliza debated, then said in a rush, "There's empty pickle jars all over Auntie Caro's kitchen."

"And he couldn't find Kool-Aid or something better?"

"No." Eliza leaned closer and confided, "Know those hot kind with red peppers in the bottom?" Keely nodded warily. "Kyler bet Gib a dollar he wouldn't take a drink." A grudging sort of admiration lit Eliza's blue eyes. "But Gib showed him. He drank the *whole* jar."

"No wonder he's barfing," she muttered. "Where is he now?"

Eliza shrugged her delicate shoulders, staring with acute fascination at the grass-stained toes of her white Mary Janes. One gloved finger twisted a springy ribbon on her flower basket.

Keely hated to play hardball with Kade and Skylar's stubborn daughter, but if Gib was lost, then so were the wedding rings. She whispered, "You'd better spill it, Eliza Belle, or I'll tell your mom about the plate of mints you stashed in your backpack."

Without hesitation, Eliza rattled off, "He's hiding in the empty closet at the end of the hallway with Thane, Braxton, Kyler, Hayden and Anton."

"Better that than knocking back shots of Wild Turkey in the gazebo with the other groomsmen," Ramona added with a snort.

"What!"

"Ramona!" Jessie McKay gasped.

"I'm not supposed to tell her that her brothers and male cousins are giving Jack very detailed advice on how to handle her?"

India, Jessie and Domini vehemently shook their heads no.

"I'll kick Trevor and Edgard's asses if they're in on it," Chassie assured her.

"Same goes for Carter," Macie promised.

Why had Jack needed a stiff drink? *He* wasn't stuck wearing a feather duster on his head.

"I'll find my oldest wayward son," Channing said, shifting Austin on her hip away from her pregnant belly. "Don't worry. Pickle juice is nothing. Gib has an iron gut." She offered Keely no such promise about Jack's condition. "I hope you and Jack have all girls." She sighed and kissed Austin's dark head. "They've gotta be easier than McKay boys."

"You forgetting Keely took hellraising to a whole 'nother level?" her Aunt Kimi prompted. "What goes around comes around. She's gonna get stuck with a quartet of girls exactly like her, you mark my words."

"Listen to her, Keely," Skylar said. "She predicted Kade and I would have twin girls."

Her family was already discussing when they were going to

have kids? She and Jack weren't even married yet.

Keely froze.

Married. Oh. My. God. She and Jack were really getting married. Today. In front of all these people. In—she gaped at the clock—eighteen minutes.

Keely's stomach pitched like a horse trailer caught in a prairie windstorm. The room was too hot. With too many people. Why did she have so damn many brothers? And cousins? And why had her relatives populated the place with all these noisy kids?

Sweat broke out on her brow. Her skin dried and drew tight over her bones. Muted laughter, the rustle of silky fabrics, the click of high heels on the tile; it was all too loud. The heavy scent of hairspray, perfume and flowers burned her nostrils, stuck in her throat and made it impossible for her to breathe.

Why couldn't anyone see she was suffocating?

Heedless of wrinkling the satin and lace, Keely yanked up the dress, dropped her head between her knees and sucked air deep into her lungs.

The room became momentarily still, then the crowd circled her. Gentle female hands patted her back. The feminine buzzing began again, siphoning every available ounce of oxygen and sanity.

A voice boomed, "Oh for heaven's sake, give her some air." A round of annoyed female whispers and grumbles gave away to eerie quiet as her well-meaning relatives were shooed out.

In a soothing tone, AJ said, "Keely?"

Keely lifted her head. Her BFF-sister-in-law's pregnant belly protruded in her lavender bridesmaid's gown. "You look like an anemic grape."

"Good thing Cord likes grapes. But this isn't about me and my latest McKay baby bump, so cut the crap. Is your dress too tight?"

Maybe the bodice was cutting into her oxygen supply and making her lightheaded. And paranoid.

Nope. The minute Keely sat upright, panic set in again. "I can't breathe. I can't think. I can't do this." She grabbed AJ's hand, pleading, "You've got to get me out of here."

"Where would you go?" AJ asked calmly.

"I don't know!" Keely leapt to her feet and began to pace in the large, sunny bedroom. "None of this is real. These aren't my real clothes. This isn't my real face." Her voice caught on a sob. "What is Jack gonna think when he sees me?"

AJ clasped Keely's hands. "It is you. Maybe a fancier you, but it's still Keely McKay under the layers of chiffon and silk. Jack will think the same thing he always has—you are the woman he loves and wants to spend the rest of his life with."

"Somewhere deep inside I think I know that, I just..." Keely trailed off, her heart threatening to beat right out of the lace-trimmed sweetheart neckline.

She loved Jack. Jack loved her. Simple. When had their simple declaration of that love turned into a three-ring circus, complete with clown makeup and funny shoes?

"We should've made a break for Vegas like you and Cord

did."

"It would've hurt your dad not to walk his baby girl down the aisle, K."

"Part of me understands. But I still need…"

"I know exactly what you need, sweetie, and I'll be right back with it." AJ disappeared.

Keely hoped AJ planned to dose her with Wild Turkey. After several minutes passed by, Keely realized she'd been left alone for the first time in hours. She didn't waste time contemplating her options. She needed fresh air. She cracked open the door and peeked out.

The coast was clear.

Grabbing the billowy folds of her ivory wedding dress, she took off, the cushiony carpet muffling her footfalls. At the end of the long hallway stood a narrow set of stairs, which led to the first floor and her temporary freedom.

Hallelujah.

Keely's hand had just connected with the antique brass handrail, when a deep voice behind her inquired, "Going somewhere?"

Jack.

Everything inside her jumped for joy.

Yet, Jack didn't sound particularly overjoyed to see her. In fact, he sounded downright furious.

"Answer me."

She stammered, "Uh, don't you know it's bad luck for the groom to see the bride before the wedding?"

"Yeah? It's even worse luck for the groom to see his bride making a break for it ten minutes before the ceremony is set to start."

Jack was close enough she felt his hot breath teasing her sweat-dampened neck.

"Keely, are you having second thoughts?"

"No!" She spun around so fast the veil whapped him in the face. "I just—" The words died in her mouth at his stunned expression.

Jack stayed absolutely still. Then he smiled the wicked smile that was hers alone. He captured her hand, bringing it to his lips for a gentle kiss. "You'd think by now I'd be used to the way you take my breath away every damn time I look at you, cowgirl."

Speechless didn't begin to explain Keely's emotions. Before she could articulate a single one, voices echoed up the main staircase at the other end of the hall.

Jack read her panic and pulled her into the first available room—which wasn't a room at all, but the closet Gib and his cohorts had hidden in. As soon as they were inside, Jack tugged at the string attached to the light bulb, plunging the space into darkness.

He enfolded her against his hard body and Keely sank into him, inhaling his familiar scent, subtle expensive cologne and warm man. Her man. She sighed. Her heart rate returned to normal. Everything returned to normal.

"Better?" he murmured.

"You have no idea. How did you know?"

"AJ tracked me down. But truthfully, I'd been lurking in the hallway hoping to see you."

"You weren't slamming shots of Wild Turkey with the groomsmen?"

"You heard about that?"

"Did you need liquid courage at the thought of tying yourself to me for the rest of your life, GQ?"

"No, buttercup, I had one to be polite and to keep me from ripping the damn hinges off the door to get to you."

To get to you. "You never follow the rules. Why didn't you just barge in?"

"With all those pregnant women throwing nasty looks my way?" Jack shuddered. "No thanks. Besides, your damn sisters-in-law and assorted crazy female relatives locked the damn door."

"Why?"

"'Tradition' they said."

"I wouldn't think you'd care what they said."

"I didn't. But my immediate response isn't worth repeating." His large hands tightened around her waist. "I was going crazy without you." Jack's warm lips tracked kisses across the slope of her shoulder. "I hardly slept last night, the bed seemed so big and lonely without my bed hog."

Amazing, how quickly they'd melded into one unit. Sharing living space and office space. Sharing their lives, their hopes, their dreams, their fears, their love. The only thing left was to make it legal. Seeing Jack, touching him, knowing he was as anxious as she, set her world right again.

She twisted in his arms to face him. "Just so you know, I wasn't running from you just now, I was running *to* you." The veil fluttered with her every exhalation. "Here it is, my wedding day and I feel like I'm playing dress up." Her voice dropped even lower. "I'm afraid I'll wake up and find it's not real."

Jack's hands slipped up under the veil and tenderly cupped her face. "I'm very real. It is real this time."

"Prove it. Kiss me. Please, Jack."

"No." His hands dropped to her shoulders. "Not until my ring is on your finger and I know you're mine forever."

Forever. She liked the sound of that.

He paused. "Besides, I have no idea what I'm supposed to do with the veil."

Keely laughed at his wariness. "You think the veil is bad, wait until you get a load of the hundred or so buttons on the back of this dress."

Jack groaned.

"But what I've got on underneath will be worth learning how to work a buttonhook."

He actually whimpered.

"Everyone is probably wondering where we are."

"I know. I'd say let them wonder, but I'm ready to do this thing."

"Me too."

Keely stepped out of the comfort of his arms, giddy in the knowledge in a few short minutes, she could take comfort in those strong arms every day for the rest of their lives.

"I love you, Jack. I'll meet you downstairs."

"I'll be waiting."

SLOW RIDE

Four hours later...

THIS WAS THE longest wedding reception in the history of the world. She wished it were over—which truly was saying something, since it was *her* wedding reception.

Jack leaned closer and whispered, "Stop sighing."

His warm breath sent goose bumps cascading down the right side of her body. Keely turned her head so his five o'clock shadow scraped her jaw. She closed her eyes and inhaled his familiar scent: cologne, starch on his shirt collar and the underlying hint of his heated flesh.

Jack Donohue. Her husband. She really and truly was married to this gorgeous, sexy, intense man.

Keely sighed again, not out of annoyance, but out of pure pleasure.

He smiled against her cheek. "Now that's a sigh I recognize."

"I have different sounding sighs?"

"Uh-huh. You make that one in bed after I—"

"Bringing up sex when we aren't having any just makes me cranky, Jack."

His soft chuckle tickled her ear.

"It's not funny. Why aren't we rolling around in bed nekkid right now?" she demanded in a fierce whisper. "We are married. Why are we still stuck at the reception? No one would care if we left."

He eased back to gaze into her eyes. "As much as I can't wait to roll around naked with you, if we skip out early, your dad will kill me, turning you into a widow before you've had a chance to be a wife." His voice dropped an octave and the possessive rumble vibrated through her in an electric caress. "*My* wife."

"You certainly get off on saying *my wife*."

"Yes, I do, Keely McKay *Donohue*. So go ahead and call me a Neanderthal."

"I would if it meant you'd employ some caveman tactics and drag me off to your cave. Right now?" she asked hopefully.

"God, I wish."

"Jack, I—"

The chinking of silverware hitting glassware crescendoed. Knowing what the crowd of family and friends wanted, Keely twined her arms around Jack's neck and gave him a long, wet, tongue-tangling kiss that probably caused some guests to squirm in their seats. She didn't give a damn. It was her wedding day. If she wanted to make out with her husband, she damn well would.

When they broke apart, Jack murmured, "Two more hours and I swear we're outta here."

"I'm holding you to that."

"I'd expect nothing less, buttercup."

"So where are we going in one hour and fifty-nine minutes?"

He kissed her temple and said, "It's a surprise," for the millionth time. Then his brother Justin snagged his attention and he turned away.

Sneaky-ass tease. Jack hadn't told her where they were spending their two-week island honeymoon beyond the cryptic hint that she only needed to pack beachwear—preferably a dozen skimpy bikinis.

Normally he'd spill his guts if she bribed him with unlimited, no-strings-attached sexual favors. But this time, the stubborn man wouldn't budge.

After the Twin Pines banquet workers cleared the dinner plates, the head table was disassembled to make room for the wedding dance and members of the wedding party were relocated. Which would've been fine with her, if she and Jack hadn't ended up on opposite sides of the dance floor.

A hard bump connected with her hip as AJ McKay—her best friend, matron of honor and sister-in-law—sidled up beside her. "Why the frowny face, Mrs. Donohue?"

She plastered on a fake grin. "Better?"

"No, that's actually worse. What's up? You seem jumpy."

Would she sound like a horny ho-bag if she admitted all she could think about was jumping her husband? Wait. Could she even *be* a ho-bag if she was obsessed about having nonstop, shake-the-barn-rafters sex with the man she'd just pledged the rest of her life to?

"Granted, we're all anxious. It's been a crazy couple of weeks," AJ said, breaking Keely's thoughts. "Four different family members having bouts of false labor during your bridal shower. The bachelorette party. I think Ramona is still hungover."

Everyone had been shocked at how tame former wild child Keely McKay's bachelorette party had played out last weekend. Not a lot of takers for a tequila shooting contest besides her cousin Ramona when the majority of Keely's sisters-in-law and female family members were knocked up. But truthfully, not reverting to her formerly rowdy ways—even for one night—had been a huge relief.

Screeching feedback from the microphone distorted the air.

"Sorry about that," JC Blackwell said from the stage. "The band is set up and we're ready to kick off the weddin' dance. So can I get Carson and Keely up here? We'll start out with the father-daughter dance. Hey, you know, in all the years I've been doin' this, that's the first time I've ever said that at a

McKay wedding."

Laughter rang out as Keely met her father in the center of the dance floor.

He squinted at her.

"What?"

"You've got a funny look on your face, girlie. Aw hell, you ain't gonna cry again, are you?"

"Maybe." She playfully tugged on the silky silver handkerchief poking out of the front pocket of his suit. "At least you're prepared if I do begin to bawl."

He muttered, "Don't know why I have to wear this fancy-ass piece of crap. It's worthless."

Keely laughed.

The band started a cover of Kenny Chesney's "There Goes My Life" and her dad twirled her around and around the dance floor like he had when she was five years old. She looked at him suspiciously.

"What?"

"Have you been drinkin'?"

"Yep. Ain't every day a man gives away his daughter. His only daughter."

Damn him. She was trying so hard not to cry. "Daddy—"

"We dancin'?" he asked gruffly. "Or talkin'?"

"Dancing. Definitely." And she let him twirl her all he wanted.

When the dance ended and he hugged her in such a public display of affection, she knew he'd been hitting the bottle.

When he released her and motioned for JC to bring the microphone to him, Keely thought her father might actually be hammered. Her dad. Making a speech. In front of over two hundred people.

He held her hand and cleared his throat. "The McKay Ranch had been in existence for almost a hundred years when this little gal made an appearance. My brothers and me never considered what havoc this little spitfire would cause in all our lives and our future."

More laughter.

Keely's stomach clenched. She desperately wanted Jack by her side as support in case her father's impromptu speech somehow embarrassed her.

"Our beautiful Keely was the only girl for a long time. But with the arrival of more darlin' little girls into the McKay family the last few years"—he winked and waved at his granddaughters, Liesl, Oxsana and Sasha—"me'n my brothers know that times are changin' and these girls deserve to have an equal part in the McKay Ranch if they choose to.

"So we've restructured the way we're doin' things and… Hell, it'll be easier to show you. Hang on a second." He released Keely's hand and rooted in the inside pocket of his suit coat. He held out a folded piece of paper.

Keely gave him a blank look.

"Go on, girlie. Open it up."

With shaking hands, Keely unfolded the legal document and she scanned the words. She reread it twice before she met her father's bright eyes. "Daddy, are you serious?"

"Yep."

The McKay Ranch had deeded Keely and Jack Donohue acreage. Beyond shocked, beyond touched, she couldn't utter a single word.

Carson whirled around, searching the crowd. "Donohue? Where are you?"

Jack stepped forward and wrapped his arm around Keely's waist before he peered at the document. He looked at Keely and then Carson. "Wow. That's very generous. Thank you, sir."

"My pleasure. Though, I don't envy the headaches you're gonna have building my girl her dream house on that spot she's always had her eye on. Do you know how many dollhouses she had growin' up? I can't count all the hours she spent redecorating them."

More laughter.

Her father, the comedian. Just when she was afraid he'd keep going, Carson handed the microphone back to JC. He walked straight into the arms of Keely's mother, who stood on the edge of the dance floor, with damp cheeks and wet eyes.

JC said, "Let's give our bride and groom their first dance as husband and wife."

Jack tucked the paper inside his tux pocket and brought Keely against his body as the band began to play "So Good in Love" by George Strait.

Keely clutched him, burying her face in his neck to hide

her tears.

Jack didn't say a word. He didn't have to. He just knew what she needed and gave it to her without question.

God she loved this man.

The song ended and another slow one began. She'd specifically requested all slow songs be played first, figuring it'd be the only time she'd get to slow dance with her husband.

Sure enough, her oldest brother, Cord, tapped Jack on the shoulder during the second song. "Mind if I cut in?"

"Hell yes, I mind. Go dance with your own wife, McKay."

Okay. That was…atypical Jack behavior.

Her next oldest brother, Colby, tried to cut in, and once again, Jack refused.

Same response when her brother Colt approached them.

Same response when her brother Cam approached them.

Same response when her brother Carter approached them.

Then Jack systematically shot down all eight of her McKay cousins and all eight of her West cousins.

Puzzled by his hard stance, she whispered, "Jack. What is wrong with you?"

"I don't trust any of your redneck relatives not to hijack you for that stupid 'steal the bride' tradition. I'm letting them know the only man stealing you away tonight is me." His lips brushed her ear. "In one hour and seventeen minutes."

"Oh." That was really sort of sweet. Demented, but sweet.

Finally Jack relented and let Keely dance with his brother Justin—but only because Jack was dancing right beside them with his mother, Doro, the entire time, watching them like a hawk.

His possessive behavior didn't piss her off like it did when her hard-assed, overprotective brothers and cousins acted the same way. Although outwardly Jack was much more polished than her male relatives, inside, every inch of him screamed primal dominant male. And could she just get a *thank you, Jesus* for that fact?

After Justin handed her back to Jack, her nephews and nieces surrounded them, both intrigued and repelled by their ability to get Aunt Keely to kiss Uncle Jack simply by hitting a spoon into a glass.

She and Jack exited the dance floor and made the rounds together, chatting with wedding guests. When Keely glanced at the clock she realized only thirty minutes remained until she and Jack planned to leave.

Where was he taking her? And why had her matron of honor disappeared?

While Jack was engrossed in a conversation with Trevor and Edgard, Keely tired of waiting for AJ to materialize. She palmed the dressing room key and quickly ducked down the hallway out of Jack's sight. Maybe he wouldn't notice she was gone. Besides, she only needed a minute to ditch the ridiculously puffy underskirt—which was not enough time for any of her brothers to snatch her.

She unlocked the door to the makeshift dressing room, opening it just far enough to sneak inside. As she quietly shut the door by pressing her palms into it, she heard *squeak squeak squeak* and then, "Yes. God, yes."

"That's it, baby doll, give me one more."

Squeak squeak squeak.

Keely whirled around. Cord had AJ bent over the table with her hands gripping the edge. His pants were around his ankles and her dress was flipped up her back and… Why in the hell hadn't they heard her come in?

The *squeak squeak squeak* of the table rocking across the floor was only slightly louder than AJ's moan.

That was why.

Keely shrieked and clapped her hand over her eyes before she faced the door again. "Omigod. I did *not* just see you two boinking like bunnies during my wedding reception!"

Silence.

And the silence was worse than the squeaking and moans.

"Keely—"

She held up her hand, but didn't turn around. "Not a word, Cord. I'm leaving, but so help me God you two had better finish up fast because I need AJ's help pronto." With that, she practically ran out.

Big surprise Jack blocked the mouth of the hallway, arms crossed over his chest, one eyebrow raised, wearing his *What the fuck?* expression.

Shit. "I can explain."

"Later. Right now they want us to cut the cake." He held out his hand.

Keely threaded her fingers through his, allowing him to lead the way to the cake table.

Photos were snapped. Given their volatile past, everyone seemed disappointed when she and Jack didn't smear wedding cake all over each other's faces.

"It's time to go," he said, nibbling frosting from her fingertips.

"Okay. As soon as AJ gets done screwing—"

"Hey, guys, what's up?"

Keely looked over at her very mussed, very flushed sister-in-law. Before she shot off a snarky comment like *Besides your skirt?* Jack spoke.

"We're getting ready to leave. Can you tell me where it is?"

"What? Oh, that. Umm, it's at the senior center."

"Thank you."

Her gaze bounced between AJ and Jack. "What the hell are you two talking about?"

"Nothing to concern yourself with, sweet wife." Jack's smooch on her cheek didn't mollify her at all.

Ramona bounded up. "Now that you've cut the cake, it's gotta be close to time to throw the bouquet, right?"

"Yes. Round up all the single ladies. Maybe you could get Justin to help you track down the bachelors for the garter—"

"Not necessary," Jack inserted, "because there won't be a garter toss."

"What?" Keely stared at him with total confusion. "But that's tradition! You remove the garter—"

"Oh, I *will* be removing the garters, Mrs. Donohue, but not in front of your whole damn family."

The set to his jaw indicated this was nonnegotiable.

Bossy man.

"Soon," he added in that alpha male tone, which always made her weak-kneed.

AJ tugged on her arm. "Come on. I'll help you get changed."

As they turned the corner and started down the hallway, Keely saw her cousin Brandt McKay in a heated discussion with Jessie McKay, his former sister-in-law. Suddenly, Jessie pulled back and punched Brandt in the stomach hard enough that Brandt bent over to clutch his gut.

Keely gasped.

Jessie's angry gaze zeroed in on Keely and then she glanced at AJ who'd frozen a few steps behind. "Sorry. I didn't mean…"

"To punch Brandt in the stomach? That was an accident?"

"Umm. No. I meant to do that. I didn't mean to cause a scene and I…really have to wash my hands."

Keely's eyes stayed on Jessie, but Jessie wouldn't look at her. "Don't be too long. I'm about to throw the bouquet."

AJ unlocked the door to the dressing room and Keely followed her inside.

"I can't believe Jessie just slugged Brandt. What do you think is going on with them?"

"Nice try at distracting me, AJ, but I can't believe you and

Cord were having sex in here." Keely reached under the layers of her wedding gown and yanked off the puffy crinoline slip that'd started to itch. Ah. Much better. "How is it you get to have sex on my wedding day? And I don't? That's not fair."

"Being pregnant makes me horny. Plus Cord looks so damn good in that suit I just wanted him right then and—"

"And my brother just obliged you? During my wedding reception?"

She shrugged. "Hormones and lust are beyond my control, Keely, when it comes to my husband. And he's always up to the challenge of taking care of my every need." AJ smoothed her hands over the bulging front of her bridesmaid's dress and frowned. "Good Lord. How Cord still wants me and sees me as sexy when I look like a beached whale is a miracle." She caught Keely's gaze. "Anyway, let's get you outta that wedding dress and into your traveling clothes."

Keely stood in front of the antique boudoir mirror, fussing with the lace panel on the bodice as AJ began unhooking the hundred or so buttons running down the back of her dress. "Do you know where Jack is taking me for our honeymoon?"

"Yep."

Her mouth dropped open. "How'd you get him to tell you?"

"I volunteered to keep his car hidden so none of your overzealous relatives would decorate it with soap, shaving cream, tin cans and toilet paper," she said smugly. "That's what we were just talking about. Where I stashed it."

AJ played dirty, knowing how much Jack babied that car. But Keely had a trump card. "So, BFF, seeing you and Cord going at it like teenagers just proves how little alone time you two get these days with two point three kids, so I'll make you an offer—I'll baby-sit the boys every Saturday night for a month if you tell me where Jack is whisking me off to."

"No deal. If Jack finds out I blabbed... Well, he is much scarier than you, Keels."

The door opened.

Speak of the devil... Jack sauntered in, and once again Keely marveled at how dangerously sexy he looked in his black tux. Plus, he was sporting that wicked *get naked* grin that always caused her body to pulse with anticipation.

"Jack, you're not supposed to be in here," AJ said.

"I need to talk to my wife."

"It can wait."

"No, it can't."

"My job as her matron of honor is to help her out of her wedding dress," AJ reminded him.

Keely met Jack's eyes in the mirror. "Jack is very good at getting my clothes off, aren't you?"

"Dare I say...I'm an expert at it?"

AJ muttered, "And...that's my cue to leave."

"Lock the door and don't tell anyone where we are for at least ten minutes," Keely said as AJ fled the room.

Her body stayed perfectly still as Jack sidled in behind her.

"Only ten minutes?" He pressed a soft, warm kiss to her

nape. "I should be insulted."

"You could prove me wrong. I know firsthand that table over there is sturdy enough for whatever you've got in mind."

His eyes narrowed. "How do you know that firsthand?"

Crap. "Only because I walked in on Cord and AJ havin' a quickie."

"Ah. However, just to be clear, buttercup, there is no quickie in your immediate future."

"Then why are you in here?"

He sighed. "All you want me for is sex. I feel so cheap." His rough-skinned fingers traced the bare line of her spine down to where the buttons of her dress were undone.

"I could make you feel used too," she offered. She felt the fabric shift as Jack loosened her dress. Her skin beaded from his steady, gentle touch.

"Thanks, but no. To answer your question, I'm here to give you news."

"Good or bad?"

"Both. The bad news is I'm undressing you now. Other-wise, I won't have a chance to see the very sexy wedding night lingerie you've been teasing me with all damn day."

Keely stared at his dark head reflected in the mirror. "Why's that?"

"Because as soon as you're changed and done tossing the bouquet, we'll be hopping in the car and driving to Denver. Our flight leaves at five a.m. So we won't immediately have a wedding night, rolling around naked in bed, like you've been hinting at all damn day."

A whine arose but she squashed it. "So what's the good news?"

"I promise the wait will be worth it when we get to our honeymoon destination."

"Which is where?"

His mouth grazed her ear as he continued working the buttons. "Tahiti."

She smiled. "Tahiti is good."

"Mmm. I thought you'd like that. Especially since we'll have two weeks to roll around naked in our private villa. Or on our private beach."

She couldn't freakin' wait for two weeks alone with Jack. "What time will we get there?"

"We fly from Denver to LA, and from LA to Papeete. Tahiti is a little off the grid, so it'll take about fourteen hours. We should be there in time tomorrow night to see the sunset." He kissed the side of her neck and murmured huskily, "That was the last button. Turn around and drop the dress, Keely."

Her blood heated. Her pulse spiked. Her body went wet and soft in places, tight and hard in others. Jack could fire her up in no time flat with mere words. But that didn't mean she'd make it easy on him. Or that she wouldn't use every feminine trick in the book to get him to recant his "no quickie in your immediate future" comment.

Holding the bodice in place over her chest, she faced him.

Jack wore the hooded expression that told her he was trying very hard to keep it together and keep his hands off her.

Ooh. Snapping his control was gonna be so much fun.

Keely loosely held the dress with her left hand, giving him the occasional glimpse of her cleavage, while her right hand began to remove the bobby pins maintaining her up 'do.

"What are you doing?"

"Lettin' my hair down." The pins hit the tile floor, one at a time, each with a soft *ping*. "You like it when I let loose, don't you, Jack? And I've been coiled so tightly all day."

He said not a word, but his hands were clenched into fists at his sides. The muscles in his jaw jumped, as did the muscle in his pants.

Heh heh.

After the last pin freed her hair, she sighed as the tresses fell, knowing how Jack loved to wrap those loose waves around his hands as he fucked her. "Ah. I needed that. Now. Where were we?"

"Goddammit, Keely—"

"Oh, right, you asked me to drop the dress." She released the heavy weight of the beaded bodice and it gradually slid down her upper torso, briefly clinging to her hips before she slipped it over her thighs to pool around her feet in a pile of satin, chiffon, and lace.

Not that Jack noticed the crumpled state of her wedding dress. His gaze was firmly glued on her undergarments.

Low-cut push-up bra edged in white lace?

Check.

Ass-molding boy shorts in white spandex also edged in lace?

Check.

Satin and lace garters holding up sheer white stockings?

Check.

White satin stiletto peep-toe pumps with delicate ankle straps?

Check.

Hungry, possessive look on Jack's face?

Check.

Keely tiptoed over the heap of fabric and stopped, expecting Jack would rush her, pin her to the wall, and do all the raunchy things that were etched on his handsome face.

But the stubborn man didn't move.

So she did. She twirled and gave him her backside, swinging her hair as she threw her arms above her head and gyrated her hips. Then she peered at him over her shoulder and murmured, "You like?"

And...he was done for.

Jack's growl was her only warning before he was on her. Spinning her into his arms, smashing her mouth beneath his, kissing her frantically, one hand twisted in her hair, the other clamped on her butt.

Keely wasn't too far gone with lust not to release a little chuckle of superiority that Jack's resistance had vanished so fast upon seeing her peep-show.

He herded her until the backs of her thighs hit the table

ledge. Without missing a beat, Jack lifted her, positioning himself between her legs, continuing to gift her with the soul kisses she craved.

After he'd gotten her worked up to the point she writhed against him, he trailed his lips to her ear. "Such a cocktease you are, wife. You are going to pay for that little display. Later."

"Later? Not now?"

"No." Jack nuzzled her temple. Then his mouth followed the curve of her cheek to the corner of her smile. Keeping his eyes on hers, he lightly sank his teeth into her bottom lip before continuing the hot, wet, openmouthed kisses down the column of her throat.

Keely moaned, tempted to let her head fall back, close her eyes and lose herself in the mind-boggling way this man made her feel. But she kept her eyes on Jack as he conducted his sensual blitz. When he looked at her, a hint of devilry glinting in his eyes, she shivered.

"Cold?" he murmured as his tongue traced the lace band of her bra down the valley of her cleavage.

"Yes. You should do the gentlemanly thing and take your clothes off to use your body heat to keep me warm."

He chuckled against the upper swell of her breast. But he didn't dally. That oh-so-talented mouth progressed south-ward, slower than she liked, but chances were high they both had the same end point in mind.

Finally.

Keely's breath stalled when his hands gripped the tops of her legs and spread her thighs wider. She squirmed when Jack's tongue traced the McKay cattle brand tattooed on her hip.

And she flat out whined when he retreated.

"Better grow some patience, cowgirl. You're going to need it." He grabbed her right ankle, leisurely unbuckled the rhinestone strap and threw her shoe behind him.

She laughed. The man surprised her on so many levels. She knew a lifetime wouldn't be enough to learn everything that made him tick. "Jack. I love you."

"I know you do."

"Don't you have something to say back to me?"

"Yes." He lifted her left ankle and removed that shoe in the same manner. He stepped just out of her reach and said huskily, "Unhook the stockings."

"But…" That wasn't what she wanted to hear.

"But what?"

"But isn't that your job?" she cooed. "Divesting me of *all* my apparel?"

Jack shook his head, but his gaze remained on the satin bridal garter, centered mid-thigh, below the band of the stocking. "Unfasten them, but leave the stockings and the garters on."

Damn man was taking all the fun out of it…or was he? Keely crooked her finger. "I need to borrow your big, strong body to support myself so I don't faint dead away with all the unbridled lust you bring out in me, husband."

He grinned and said, "Laying it on a little thick, aren't you?" but he edged forward.

Keely gently set her foot on his crotch. Not as unaffected as he projected; he was totally hard. "Talk about thick." She smirked when he growled again, but she noticed he didn't even attempt to move her foot.

She popped the buttons, moving the bridal garter up over the top of the stretchy band of the stocking, and slid her stocking-clad foot up and down his erection before she switched sides.

Once the stockings were loose, Jack leaned in and kissed her. A teasing brush of his lips. A fleeting nibble of his mouth on hers as his fingers inched up her thigh in a whisper-light touch across her trembling skin. When he reached the top of the stocking, he inserted his finger inside the silky material and slowly, slowly, slowly dragged it down the length of her leg.

Keely's whole body was quivering. Tingling even. And he hadn't even started working his magic touch on all her other special tingly parts. "Jack—"

Her protest disappeared in his intense kiss.

Jack removed the other stocking with the same painstaking precision, with such drawn out eroticism, she whimpered.

He dropped to his knees.

Oh hell yeah. Now we're talkin'.

His mouth meandered up the inside of her thigh, the tantalizing touch of his hot breath, wet tongue, moist lips and the scrape of his five o'clock shadow was almost too much to bear. He latched onto the bridal garter with his teeth, snapped it once, and tugged it down her leg.

Okay, this garter removal business *was* much better in private.

One down, one to go.

She expected he'd torment her mercilessly on the other leg before pressing his mouth to her damp panties and giving her what she really wanted.

But Jack just tugged the other bridal garter off and rolled to his feet. "Done. Now get dressed so we can hit the road."

"That's *it*?"

"What? Were you expecting we'd go at it right here, right now?"

"Uh, yeah. Wasn't that the point?"

"No. I'll admit I was considering throwing you a bone after the striptease, but you were so cocksure I had no control—"

"Throwing me a bone?" she repeated. "Are you tryin' to piss me off, Jack?"

His eyebrows rose. "On our wedding day? Not likely."

"Then why won't you—"

"Pin you down on the table or on the tile floor or against the wall and screw you blind?"

"That'd work for me."

"Too bad, because it doesn't work for me."

She frowned. "You're goin' all puritan on me now that

we're married?"

"Hell no, but I don't want fast and dirty the first time we make love as husband and wife, okay? I want to take my time with you. I want it slow."

Keely stared at him for a few seconds, thrown by his PC reference to sex. "My God, GQ, sometimes you are such a girl."

There. That oughta goad him into proving his masculinity. Right now.

Probably twice.

But he laughed—a bit meanly. "Nice try. But I will not fuck you until we're alone, in a room with a huge bed, with the surf pounding in our ears and zero chance we'll be interrupted by any of your two million family members." He kissed her forehead. "And that, my sweet, sexy, horny wife, is a promise."

"Promises are meant to be broken."

"Not this one."

A challenge? She loved a challenge. Keely would do everything in her power to make him eat his words—preferably while he was eating her.

Smirking, she tucked the garter in the front pocket of his tux jacket. "If you change your mind, all you've gotta do is wave the white garter and surrender to me."

"Not happening."

She shrugged. "We'll see. Now scram so I can get dressed and we can get out of here."

THREE HOURS LATER Jack was this-goddamn-close to saying *fuck it*, pulling off to the side of the road in nowhere Wyoming and fucking Keely until she couldn't walk.

It figured his ornery cowgirl couldn't just sit back and accept that he wanted to wait. No, she'd decided to turn it into a game of make Jack sweat. Within ten miles of driving away from the wedding reception, she'd offered to give him a handjob.

He'd declined.

Then she'd offered to give him a blowjob.

He'd declined.

Then she'd asked if he minded if she took the edge off herself by masturbating.

He minded. A lot. He said as much.

But she'd just laughed, slipped her fingers beneath her sundress and proceeded to get herself off.

Twice.

God. If he didn't have any willpower now, how was he supposed to survive the next eleven hours?

"What are you thinking about?" she prompted.

As if the vixen didn't know. "How absolutely exquisite you looked today. How lucky I am. How happy I am that you married me." Jack lifted her hand and kissed her knuckles. "What are you thinking about?" She opened her mouth and he warned, "Besides sex."

"I've actually been thinking about my dad's wedding gift. It was a shock." Her frown morphed into a sneaky smile that never boded well for him. "But then again, he did give us the section of land that's closest to their house."

Jack groaned. "I knew there had to be a catch."

"It'll be handy to have Grandpa and Gran-gran so close when we have kids." She paused. "How many times did you get asked during the reception when we're gonna start a family?"

"I lost track after seventy."

Keely laughed. "I rather liked seein' you skirting the issue, Jack. But as long as we've got time to kill, maybe we ought talk about kidlets. Since it's something we haven't discussed."

The last two months since they'd set the wedding date had been a whirlwind. Opening Keely's clinic, setting up his office space in her building, meeting with his clients across the country to explain he was only changing his physical address, not the nature of his consulting business. He and Keely had been apart more than either of them liked, which was why they needed these two weeks alone.

"Okay."

"I'm thinkin' I'll want seven kids."

He nearly wrecked the car, his head whipped around so fast. "Seven? Are you fucking serious?"

"Yep. That's only one more than Cam and Domini have, and they're doin' fine."

"Their house and their lives are a goddamn zoo, Keely."

When she smirked, he realized he'd been had. "Very funny."

"But I do think we could handle six."

"No way."

"Fine. How many do you want?" she demanded.

"Two."

"Two? That's it? I already feel bad for our two poor babies, practically raised alone." She made the most pitiful-sounding sigh.

Jack rolled his eyes. "Last time I checked there were almost twenty-seven McKay and West cousins for Jack Junior and Little Keely to play with. That's plenty."

"Fine. Five kids."

"Nope. But I'd agree to three."

"Four."

"We'll see." Four ankle biters sounded good to him, but he had to keep some negotiating power with his wife.

His wife who'd gotten very quiet all of a sudden.

"Keely? You okay?"

Her hand tightened around his. "Just thinking. As much as I wanna have a ton of kids with you, not right away, okay? I want you all to myself for a while first."

Keely's sweetness always surprised him, always moved him, always humbled him. "Deal."

"But I definitely think we should get lots of baby-making practice in. Starting now."

"You aren't going to give this up, are you?"

"Not until you give in."

"I will gladly give in to you as soon as we hit the villa. Until then—"

"Until then you're giving me an excuse to relive my most memorable sexual encounters. Great idea." Keely's eyes took on an unholy gleam before she looked away.

The car went silent. Except for her occasional sighs.

Sighs he recognized.

This was driving him fucking insane. Which sexual encounters was she reliving? She'd better not be thinking about any man other than him. Ever.

"You do make such a sexy sounding rumble when you're jealous, Jack. It's cute."

"Cute?" His hands tightened on the steering wheel. "Fuck that. I'm not cute."

"True. You're definitely too hot to merely be cute." Keely peeled his fingers free from the steering wheel and clasped his hand in hers, setting their joined hands on her lap. "And so you know, husband, I was thinking of you, because I completely forgot every man after the first time you touched me."

"Such a silver-tongued cowgirl." Jack relaxed because she knew just how to soothe him. "What memory were you reliving?" So much for his insistence they forgo discussions about sex.

"The one after our fake engagement party. When you just..." She sighed. "You rocked my world, GQ."

It'd been a hard and fast encounter, as they'd both been drunk on the lust that'd shimmered between them for eleven years. Lust that'd finally hit the boiling point. He'd taken her on the floor of her apartment, which yeah, the I-need-you-right-fucking-now feeling was hot as hell, pinning her to the carpet and fucking her brains out. Although, he still held some regret that's how their first time together had played out.

Is that why you're so insistent on doing this differently?

"And then I got to thinking about how we christened my office at the clinic."

An image of Keely, stripped naked and spread out on the top of her desk, flashed in his mind. That'd been a hot tryst, mostly because it was so unexpected. His cowgirl certainly liked to mix things up. He murmured, "And then we christened my office." As soon as they'd caught their breath, she'd crooked her finger and led them to his office, where she'd draped herself over his drafting table and he'd nailed her from behind. Then they'd gone at it in the conference room.

Dammit. Now he was getting hard.

He glanced at her and realized while he'd been reliving the Jack and Keely sex show, she'd dropped their joined hands between her legs and was covertly rubbing his hand right where she wanted it. He stiffened his fingers and slid them free of her grasp. "Nice try."

"But we were sharing, Jack," she cooed. "Connecting."

"You are trying to connect my fingers with something, all right," he said dryly.

Keely let loose the deep throaty laughter that made him think of slamming body parts and sweat-soaked sheets.

Damn her. He was still getting hard.

"But you know which one of our many, many, many, *many* times of getting down and dirty sticks out in my mind?"

Jack had gotten stuck on the many, many, many, *many* times portion of her question. "Ah. No, but I'm sure you'll tell me. In detail. In explicit detail."

"Last month. When you'd been gone for three weeks. I heard you running up the stairs to the apartment. You dropped everything you were carrying in front of the door and kissed me, such a deliciously long, slow kiss. Then you whispered, 'I love you' and took me to bed. And we stayed in bed the entire day. Twenty-four whole hours of mad, passionate love, wrapped together, napping, only to wake up and go at it again. It was amazing."

"I agree. It was amazing."

She fell silent, which surprised him. But he didn't push it. Then she said, "Lemme see your left hand."

"Why?"

"I just have this need to look at your wedding band, so I know this isn't some kind of dream and we really are married."

"Seems surreal, doesn't it?" Jack held his hand across the console.

Keely turned the ring on his finger. "Will it take some time for you to get used to wearing it?"

"I'm already used to it. It's never coming off."

She smiled. "So you like it?"

That she'd managed to keep the design and style of his

wedding band a secret from him was a miracle for her, his little hater of secrets. "It's perfect. Why?"

"I thought it might bother you I didn't try to match them."

The wide band wasn't too feminine or too plain. It wasn't white gold like hers, but platinum. "Keely. I love it. It shows how different we are but how well we fit together."

"Well, that's a relief."

Jack's thumb swept across her new wedding band, comprised of diamonds and sapphires, nestled beneath her eleven-karat diamond engagement ring. "Do you like yours?"

"It's really flashy, so of course I adore it."

"The sapphires reminded me of your eyes."

"Such a flatterer, but don't stop. You could start talking about my other physical attributes. I could strip nekkid if you need a reminder of what my body looks like without such constricting clothing."

Jack laughed. "Nice try."

Comfortable silence fell between them for several miles. Then she yawned.

"If you're tired, go ahead and sleep. I'll wake you when we get to Denver."

"Are we stopping at the condo before the airport?"

"No."

Keely sighed. "Damn. There goes my plan to carry you over the threshold and ravish you in your former bachelor pad."

"There will be plenty of time for ravishment in Tahiti." He

kissed the back of her hand again. "Get some rest."

"How am I supposed to change your mind about doing the nasty with me as soon as possible if I'm snoring?" She dropped his hand and turned in her seat to run her fingers through his hair. "So let's talk about all the places I'm gonna try and seduce you before our toes hit the sand."

Jack said, "Not a good idea," even as his cock pressed against his zipper, arguing it was the greatest idea in the history of the world.

This was going to be a long drive.

SIX HOURS LATER Jack was once again this-goddamn-close to saying *fuck it*, pulling Keely into the bathroom in the first class section of the airplane and fucking her until she couldn't walk.

Within ten minutes of passing through security at the Denver airport, she'd suggested they test out the private rooms in the VIP lounge.

He'd declined.

Then she'd suggested they hook up in one of the family-friendly bathrooms in preparation for joining the mile-high club on the flight to LA.

He'd declined.

It appeared she'd given up seducing him during the flight to LA, until they reached LAX and she'd started in again.

Within ten minutes of reaching their gate, she'd begun whispering her fantasies, which seemed to include a lot of lube and different kinds of rope.

But by the time they'd settled in for the final flight to the island, Keely's eyes were drooping. Her raunchy sexual suggestions had tapered off, focusing on soft pillows and cool sheets rather than vibrating marital aids and zero inhibitions.

As soon as they were airborne, she'd curled her body into his and had fallen fast asleep.

And in that moment, when it was just the two of them, snuggled together forty thousand feet in the air, Jack finally felt like they were married. That she belonged to him and he belonged to her.

The vows and the ceremony and the exchange of rings and the reception had been great and all…yet, he'd never understood before that the wedding had been for their family and friends—public proof of their commitment to each other.

So in Jack's mind, the honeymoon was the place to offer his private commitment to Keely. To look her in the eye, with no interruptions and no distractions, and let her know that he planned on loving her every day for the rest of his life.

That's why he'd been so adamant about them waiting to make love—because they'd never get another first time as husband and wife and he wanted it to be meaningful. Special. Maybe even magical.

You're such a girl, GQ.

But now he was worried. Had he built up the union of

bodies, spirits and lives to the point it'd be a big letdown for them both?

Probably. He was prone to analyze stuff to death. Nothing he could do about it now—he'd begun to regret taking such a rigid stance. He'd make it up to her. Jack rested his chin on the top of Keely's head, losing himself in the sweet lilac scent of her hair and drifted off.

They were both groggy when the plane finally landed.

The heat and the confusion about transportation made them both cranky. Rather than snipe at each other, they stayed quiet, lost in their own thoughts.

As soon as they reached the patio of the private villa, Jack pulled her into his arms and whispered, "We're here. You know what that means, don't you?" He expected she'd laugh the sultry sound that always made him hard, and drag him inside with a cheeky, *Let the rolling around nekkid begin.* He didn't expect her to disentangle from his arms and step back.

Way back.

"That means we're at the beach, Einstein."

Jack squinted at her. Dammit. Sarcastic, lashing-out Keely stood in front of him, which meant he'd somehow hurt her feelings.

Gee, ya think? You totally fucked yourself with your sexy wife, my friend, and not in a good way.

He had to figure out what to do, and fast. Charming his way back into her good graces, warred with his male instinct to just fuck his way back into her good graces. Maybe a combination of both would work? He grinned, stepped forward and took her hand, kissing the knuckle above her wedding ring. "I know it's been a long day. But if you can give me ten minutes—"

Once again she retreated. "Take as long as you want. In fact, take all night. There's no hurry, right? We've got two weeks."

"But I thought…"

"What? That I would just strip right here, right now, and wait for you to take me by the hand so you could make sweet, sweet love to me on a bed of fucking rose petals?" she demanded. "Wrong, bucko. I wouldn't have sex with you right now if you begged me."

His mouth dropped open. "What the hell?"

"In fact, I feel a headache coming on. A bad one."

"Keely—"

"Or maybe I have to wash my hair." She started humming "Wash That Man Right Outta My Hair" from *South Pacific*.

Unreal.

Sometimes she was such a pain in the ass. "I swear to God if this—"

"Or maybe I'm just too damn tired. It'll probably take me a couple of days to catch up on my sleep, bein's I'm jetlagged and all. *Days*, husband, in which you can do anything you want…with the exception of one thing."

Oh no, she wouldn't.

Oh yes, she would. With absolute glee.

She smirked. "I hear the fishing is good this time of year."

Do not yell at her on your wedding day.

Jack was trying to keep his cool, when he remembered something. He casually reached into his pants pocket, pulled out the white garter and waved it at her.

Keely looked at it, then at him, and laughed. *Laughed.* She said, "Nice try," and sauntered off toward the beach.

There was some serious groveling in his immediate future. Now he really had to set the stage, and prove to her…what?

Hell if he knew. But he'd gone this far; he couldn't back down now.

Jack dragged the two hundred suitcases into the main living area. He barely gave the space a second glance as he booked it to the massive master bedroom to make sure his specific requests had been filled.

Bouquets of fragrant flowers.

Check.

Dozens of candles.

Check.

Four bottles of champagne.

Check.

Chocolate and raspberry sauce.

Check.

Silken scarves.

Check.

Batteries.

Check.

He stared at the set-up until frustration set in. He was a goddamn engineer, for fuck's sake. He sucked at this stuff. But this was the exact romantic scenario he'd envisioned and it'd been perfectly executed. So why did it look...wrong?

Because Keely isn't here. Why in the hell did you think she would want this anyway?

When had he stopped taking into account what *she* wanted?

Jesus. He was a fucking moron.

He swallowed his pride and tracked her down. And for a minute, he just stopped and stared at the woman he'd married.

What a magnificent picture she made, standing barefoot at the edge of the ocean, wind blowing through her glossy dark hair as the last rays of sunlight danced across her skin, bathing her in a golden glow.

Luckily she didn't jerk away when he touched her. She murmured, "Beautiful, isn't it?"

"Stunning. And the scenery ain't bad either."

She leaned into his chest and sighed.

They remained locked together, waves lapping at their bare feet, gazing across the horizon until the sun disappeared and darkness surrounded them.

Finally she turned and gazed at him with those sapphire eyes that seemed to have a direct conduit to his soul.

All Jack's thoughts, fears, plans, and words of devotion vanished. So he said the first thing that popped into his head. "Keely. I love you."

"I know you do."

He supposed he deserved that. "I don't want to fuck this up."

"I know that too."

"Maybe you think it's lame that I wanted to wait to make love to you in such a…traditional way, when we've already had sex in every conceivable position and in some pretty inconceivable locations. I thought I'd try to be…"

"What? High-handed? Showing me who's boss in our marriage from the get-go?"

"No. I wanted to give you romance." He tucked a piece of hair behind her ear. "You deserve that on your wedding night."

She drilled him in the chest with her finger. "No, Jack-ass, I deserve a say in what happens on *our* wedding night. You don't get to make a decision and just expect me to fall in line with it."

"I agree. I'm sorry."

His capitulation seemed to surprise her and her smartass comment, "You were fully aware I'm not a shrinking violet—" ended abruptly. She said, "Oh. Well. Okay."

"So am I forgiven for being a jackass?"

"Maybe. But you have to make it up to me."

"Anything you want. Name it."

"Happily for you, GQ, I'm all in for making love to my husband, in a big, soft bed, with the sounds of the surf pounding in the background and no interruptions." She poked him in the chest again. "You dodged a bullet this time. Next time I won't be so accommodating."

"So noted."

Keely stared at him thoughtfully again.

"What?"

"Did you really think I'd love you more if you gave me silk sheets, flowers and candlelight?"

He honestly didn't know what to say.

"Jack. You already gave me your heart. That's all I ever wanted. That's all I need."

Might make him a pussy, but he felt tears spring to his eyes. He could barely choke out, "I can't live without you."

"Lucky thing you don't have to."

"Promise?"

"I promise." Keely stood on her tiptoes and kissed him. "Now will you please take me to bed? I've heard married sex is pretty hot."

Laughing, Jack swept her into his arms and started toward the villa. But he didn't make it far before he stopped and set her back on her feet.

"Oh, for Christsake, Jack, what now?"

He put his mouth on her ear, loving how it always caused her to tremble. Loving her whimpering sigh. "Ever rolled around naked on a beach?"

"Ah. No. Have you?"

"No."

"That'd be a first for both of us."

"That would be pretty goddamned romantic."

They looked at each other. Grinned at each other.

Keely said, "First one undressed—"

"Gets to be on top," Jack finished as she started stripping.

"And also gets to decide if it's hard and fast or slow and sweet," she added.

"Deal."

Keely won. She had less clothing on than he did. But truthfully, the first rays of moonlight reflecting off all her mouthwatering curves distracted him.

That, and the fact she still wore that sexy white wedding lingerie beneath her sundress.

Damn.

She tackled him. Pinned him. Kissed him. Owned him completely. And when they were joined in body, as well as in their hearts, Jack knew this woman would give him the ride of his life.

ALL KNOCKED UP

LORELEI JAMES

Wonder how crazy a hormonal pregnant Keely might act? Here's an excerpt from *All Knocked Up*, the short story included in the *Short Rides* Anthology that takes place four years after *Slow Ride.*

ONE

ALL KNOCKED UP

Keely—seven months pregnant…

KEELY WEST MCKAY Donohue had this pregnancy thing down pat.

Well, except for the occasional glitches when her heightened emotional state hit overload and she had a teeny, tiny, barely noticeable…episode or two.

Most of those incidents hadn't really been her fault.

Like when the grocery store had run out of her brand of laundry soap *again* and she'd attempted to express her displeasure to the manager. But he'd refused to listen to reason, calling her consumer's request a crazy woman's rant, *puh-lease*—she hadn't even hit rant stage. Then the weasel had barricaded himself in his office, had her escorted from the premises by a pimply fifteen-year-old and banned her from the store for life. Luckily, the other grocery store in town had been much more accommodating. They'd even assigned her a shopping assistant to personally escort her through the store every time she showed up.

And Jack could've prevented the incident last month if he'd just taken her out for finger steaks like she'd asked him to. His refusal to understand the depth of her craving had forced her to cook the yummy bits of breaded and fried steak herself. So, it wasn't completely her fault that she'd accidentally started a small grease fire in the kitchen and she'd had to call the fire department. The fire department in turn had called the local ambulance crew, and they had contacted her brother Cam—a Crook County Deputy—who had called her entire family. Except no one had remembered to call her husband. So when Jack had come home after work to see the driveway filled with emergency vehicles and McKays, he'd lost his mind.

She'd had to spray him down with the hose to cool him off. Then she'd really caught hell for ruining his bajillion-dollar, triple-worsted wool suit crafted out of special sheep butt hairs or some such. And people claimed she was on edge during this pregnancy?

Besides, Jack had it easy. His job as her baby daddy entailed three things:

Sucking it up and listening to her every pregnancy complaint like she was reciting secret stock tips.

Keeping her fed and never ever *ever* mentioning the amount of food she consumed on a daily basis.

Fulfilling her sexual needs whenever and wherever she wanted; or keeping his dick far away from her on those bad pregnancy days she suspected she'd chop it off if he showed it to her. Happily those days were mostly behind them now.

Not such a hard list. So why was he dragging his loafers on getting on with checking off task number three today?

Keely had even given him a choice on where he could perform his husbandly duties. While she waited for him to choose, she studied her hot hunk of manflesh. The man defined sexy—who could blame her for wanting to jump his bones all the damn time? His dark hair was disheveled from constantly running his fingers through it. His silk paisley tie remained neatly knotted and he hadn't taken off his suit jacket, which in her mind meant he hadn't really started to work yet. So this was the perfect time for a break. Besides, Jack never really meant *no*.

"Come on, Jack."

"No."

"I'll make it worth your while," she said, adding a purring

rowr.

"That's what I'm afraid of," Jack said, without looking away from his computer screen. "And stop staring at my crotch to see if I'm getting hard," he warned her.

"Just tell me if your boxers are getting tight?"

"No."

"Why not?"

"Because A, I'm thinking about work not sex, and if you want to see me before midnight, which isn't likely, you'll find a way to entertain yourself and let me finish this. B, if I do take your offer to bend you over the conference table and fuck you until you scream, guaranteed one of your ten billion family members will decide to pop in and interrupt us. *Again.*"

Keely crossed her arms over her chest trying not to feel self-conscious. She could almost rest them on her protruding belly. "That was not my fault. I cannot control my family, Jack."

"I know that only too well," he muttered. "Besides, don't you have a client scheduled?"

"She had to cancel." That's when she knew she should've lied. He'd see her offer as a way to kill time. When in actuality, she saw it as a chance to revisit their spontaneous pre-pregnancy trysts for the first time in what seemed like weeks.

Jack stopped typing and looked at her sharply. "Just because you're bored doesn't mean I am."

Bored? Fuck that and fuck you too, buddy. Or better yet, I wouldn't fuck you right now if you begged me. In fact… Then just like that surly girl disappeared and weepy woman took her place.

Awesome. She hadn't run this hot and cold even as a teenager. She hated that a curt word or a scowl from him set her off into a fit of rage or a river of tears. Yet she was sick of him and everyone else muttering about her out-of-whack hormones.

So she opted to take the high road for a change. "Sorry to interrupt you." Keely pushed off the doorframe and pulled the door shut behind her. Not slamming it. Point for her.

But Jack didn't chase her down.

That thought caused a pang of sadness. But it also steeled her determination to do something besides wait around for him.

Keely grabbed her things from her office. Although it was only three-thirty, she shut off the lights and locked the building.

Once she was in her Escalade tooling down the road, she realized she didn't want to go home. As social as her life was living amongst her assorted McKay and West relatives, she didn't want to hang out with any of them.

The baby performed a kick/karate chop maneuver and she rubbed a hand over her belly. "Guess you're fine with it bein' you and me, huh baby D? What should we do? Daddy forbids horseback riding. No more putzing around on the ATV either."

She could go to Ziggy's—see who was celebrating an early

happy hour. Throw some darts. Play some pool. But then again…her body weight balance had shifted so much in the last few months that she sucked at darts. Her oversized belly made it impossible to lean over a pool table to make a decent shot.

On impulse she drove to Spearfish.

She wandered around Walmart. Annoyed with herself for being lonely but not wanting any company. Wanting this baby out so badly, but scared to death for it to actually come out. Then the baby did a full belly roll inside her that took her breath away, forcing her to rest on a porch swing in the lawn and garden department.

As she rocked, her thoughts wandered to Jack. First time he'd been snappish with her for a while. He'd been solicitous lately—to the point she suspected the man was walking on egg shells around her.

Can you blame him after your meltdown two weeks ago?

That wasn't her fault. The stupid mixer had gotten stuck and sprayed red velvet cake batter everywhere. What woman wouldn't have thrown it off the deck and beat it to smithereens with a sledge hammer?

But Jack didn't think her behavior was normal. He'd locked up all the power tools in the shed and refused to give her a key to the new paddle lock.

So maybe she'd had a few crazy moments. But instead of fighting back, Jack had become gentle with her. Not that she wanted him to be a dick, but he hadn't been acting like the

Jack she knew and loved.

"Ma'am? Are you all right?"

Startled out of her brooding, Keely glanced up at the young Walmart employee. "I just felt a little dizzy and needed to sit."

"Okay." His gaze slid to the cart parked alongside the garden hose display. A cart filled with bags of candy and potato chips. Three liters of strawberry soda. A tube of KY. And two containers of Brussels sprouts. "Is that your cart? Because I can take it up to the checkout for you."

She looked him in the eye and lied. "I have no idea whose cart that is. It was there when I sat down."

"Oh. I'll just move it out of your way then."

She sighed. So much for sneaking junk food into the house. But her Gestapo husband would've confiscated it anyway and lectured her on bad eating habits. He found no humor in her pointing out that her cravings weren't clichéd like pickles and ice cream.

So it was the first time she'd ever left Walmart empty-handed.

Hungry—*again*—Keely stopped into a sports bar for a burger and ordered a salad, rather than a mountain of French fries. With her feet up on the bench seat, she watched the news and *Wheel of Fortune*. When she glanced at the clock, she realized she'd managed to kill three hours since she'd left the office.

But she still didn't want to go home.

She checked the newspaper for movie show times. Two

movies she'd never convince Jack to see were playing. Perfect way to entertain herself.

In the nearly empty theater she chose a seat where she could put her feet up. By the time the movie ended, her restlessness had abated and even baby D had settled down. So she opted to make it a double feature. For the second movie she armed herself with a jumbo bucket of popcorn slathered with butter, an extra-large box of Sugar Babies and a caffeine-free soda.

With her mood lighter after the sappy love story and an action flick where the hero had blown up a shit ton of stuff, she sang along with the country tunes on the radio as she drove home. So she didn't hear the siren behind her, but she sure noticed the flashing lights in her rearview mirror.

So much for her good mood.

Keely watched as her brother Cam got out of the deputy's car. By the time he reached her she'd rolled the window down. She felt her own panic rise when she saw the panic on his face. "Cam. What's wrong?"

"Jesus Christ, Keely. Are you okay?"

"Yes, I'm okay. Why wouldn't I be?"

"Because Jack's been going out of his goddamned mind the last four hours trying to track you down." He stuck his head in the window. "Where's your cell phone?"

"I don't know. I must've left the house without it. Or left it at the office."

"You are a pregnant woman. You need to have that phone

on you at all times, do you hear me?"

Enough. She was too damn old for another ass-chewing session, especially when she had to pee again. "Is that some kind of Crook County law I wasn't aware of, Deputy? Are you gonna write me a fucking ticket for not having my cell phone on my person?"

"Don't be a smart ass."

"Don't be a pain in my ass," she shot back. "And I don't need a goddamn lecture from you—"

"Yes, you do, when your husband has called the entire family to find out where the hell you are! He's worried sick, Keely. Are you really blaming him when you've been out of contact for hours?"

Her mouth dropped open. "Are you kiddin' me? I went to the movies after my husband *told* me to leave him alone so he could work! And then he has the balls to act all concerned, like it's my fault? Bullshit." She glared at Cam. "Not only did the bastard call my family to tattle on me, he called you and put out a BOLO on me too? Un-fucking-believable. He's really gonna wish he hadn't done that when I use a croquet mallet on his goddamned laptop and cell phone." Just thinking about beating the fuck out of his precious electronics made her almost giddy.

Cam retreated from the car window. "Keely. Hon. Just chill out."

"What?"

"The look on your face…"

"Is what?" she demanded.

He blurted, "Really freakin' close to evil," and took two steps back from the door so she couldn't take a swing at him. "Remember. This has all been a misunderstanding. You're safe. That's all that matters. Why don't I call Jack and tell him—"

"You'd be better off calling a fucking ambulance because I'm gonna kick his ass when I get home."

Keely rolled up the window and sped off.

If her brother wanted to give her a speeding ticket, fine. But he could damn well do it in her driveway.

JACK PACED ON the front porch.

When he saw the lights of Keely's car, he could finally breathe. He'd nearly gone bald the last four hours, pulling out his hair, desperately trying not to think of worst-case scenarios.

Cam had warned him Keely was mad—really mad, boiling mad, mad like he'd never seen her. But Jack wasn't worried. Her pregnancy mood swings were so erratic she might be whistling a happy tune after she'd had time to think on the drive home about her inconsiderate behavior. She might even throw herself into his arms with a tearful apology.

He plastered on a smile, prepared to be magnanimous.

But the door to the Escalade was thrown open so hard the

metal supports should've bent backward. Her boots hit the pavement before he could offer to help her out. Then she slammed the driver's door with enough force the entire car shook.

But it was nothing compared to how hard Keely shook.

Shit. "Keely—"

"Not a fucking word, Jack-ass. I'm so pissed off at you right now you'd better be glad I actually came home."

He took a step toward her and she growled. His wife actually fucking growled at him.

This was not good.

"Last warning to back off. I've had to pee since I left Spear-fish and getting pulled over by my brother has just made it worse…and that's your fault too." She stomped up the stairs.

Undeterred, he followed her. "Do you have any idea—"

Keely whipped around so fast he didn't have time to duck the blow from her purse. A purse she was now swinging around like a mace. He was so shocked at the vicious expression on her face that he didn't manage to dodge the second or third blow.

"Jesus, Keely. Will you knock it off?"

The next time she swung, he grabbed the strap and tugged the pink zebra cowhide bludgeoning tool from her fingers.

"Fine, have it," she yelled. "It wasn't doin' enough damage to you to suit me anyway." She stepped back and braced her hand against the house.

"Come on, Keely. Can we please talk about this?"

"No."

Count to ten. "I'm serious."

"So am I." She jammed her heel into the bootjack and removed her right boot.

"Can you please try and be reasonable?"

"Reasonable?" she repeated. "You wanna talk about bein' reasonable? You're the one who told me to buzz off and leave you alone to work."

"You took that out of context."

"Bullshit." Keely removed her other boot. "You said you wouldn't be home until midnight and I should find something to do to entertain myself."

Had he really said that?

"So are you all fired up because I wasn't standing on the porch holding your pipe and slippers to welcome you home?"

"Like that'd ever happen."

Keely growled at him again.

"Maybe I did mention I might be working late. But that doesn't change the fact that I couldn't get ahold of you when my workday ended."

"Since when am I at your beck and call, Jack Donohue?"

Where the hell had that come from? "You have to admit it's pretty irresponsible for you—a pregnant woman in a rural area—to forget your phone. What if you'd had car trouble?" he demanded.

"Then my brother, who was scouring the county for me, could've given me a ride home since you called the fucking *sheriff's* office like I was a runaway wife. I absolutely cannot believe you'd—"

"Keely. Calm down."

"Calm down?" She reached for her boot. "The fuck I will!"

The first one missed him, but the second boot hit him square in the shin. "Goddammit, that's enough!"

"No it's not! You have no idea how furious I am right now." Keely picked up a potted plant and started toward him. "You humiliated me in front of my whole family, Jack. And no doubt you'll blame this, like you blame everything else, on my out-of-control pregnancy hormones!"

"Trust me, buttercup, this psycho redneck behavior is one hundred percent you, and has nothing to do with the baby—" was all he got out before she hurled the flower pot at his head. "I cannot fucking believe you just did that."

"Then you'd better not come into the kitchen because knives are a lot harder to duck, asswipe." Keely stormed into the house. She slammed the door and he heard the snick of the lock as she locked him out.

Locked out. Of his own goddamned house.

Jack yelled, "Real mature, Keely."

Yeah, real mature yelling at your pregnant wife.

He slumped into the closest chair.

How had this escalated to this point?

You overreacted.

Okay, maybe the call to Cam had been unnecessary. But Keely didn't really believe that he'd called her family to find out where she was as some attempt at humiliation? He'd never do that to her. Jack knew how hard she'd struggled not to be seen as the baby who needed constant supervision and protection. But he'd been frantic because it was so unlike her to be incommunicado for that long. Wanting to know where she was wasn't a control thing. He missed her, and yeah, he'd felt guilty for snapping at her and blowing her off. He'd initially called her to tell her he'd finished work early because he wanted to spend time with her. But it'd turned into full-blown panic at hour three.

All he could do now was give her time to calm down. After being married for almost four years he ought to know a way to fix this.

Grovel.

Like hell. He ought to spank her.

Jack swept up the dirt and broken pot. He dug in her purse for her house keys and ended up finding her cell phone—her completely dead cell phone.

At least she'd had the phone with her.

Like that would matter now.

After he'd let himself inside, he wandered into the kitchen. He washed his hands and face, and eyed the butcher block for missing knives.

Then he wandered through the rest of the main level. Keely wasn't in the bathroom, den, living room, dining room or out on the back deck. He scaled the stairs to the second floor. Not in the nursery. Or the other three bedrooms.

The door at the end of the hallway, which led to their bedroom suite, was shut.

Probably locked.

Too bad. He'd kick the damn door in if he had to.

But it wasn't locked.

Jack stepped inside the moonlit room and froze when he saw Keely standing by the big bay window.

She wore a nearly see-through white cotton nightgown that made her look like a goddess in the moon's silvery glow. The way her dark hair trailed down her back, the swell of her abdomen and the heavier weight of her breasts only added fuel to the fire of lust burning inside him.

That's when he knew what she needed—what they both needed.

He moved in front of her and trapped her gorgeous face in his hands, tilting her head to meet his gaze. Then his mouth crashed down on hers and he kissed her with every ounce of passion and hunger she aroused in him just by existing.

Keely didn't deny his kiss or fight him, except to grab his shirt to pull him closer. They kissed crazily; mouths avid, bodies straining.

Jack herded her toward the bed. He broke the kiss, sliding his mouth to her ear. "Keely. I love you. So goddamned much. And I need you. Now. Like this."

"Yes. God, please."

He lifted the nightgown over her head. He filled his hands with her breasts and teased her neck with open-mouthed kisses and tiny sucking bites.

She arched into him and moaned.

"Sit," he ordered and inserted himself between her thighs. His hands followed the contour of her belly, amazed at how her body grew and changed every day. "So beautiful," he murmured. "Every inch of you."

"Jack, I—"

He took her mouth again.

But sneaky Keely wrested control, her sensual kisses destroying him while she unbuttoned his shirt. Her hands raced over his torso, her fingers digging into his flesh. Then her mouth was on his chest, her tongue flicking his nipples between soft, suctioning kisses.

His blood pounded so hard even his skin throbbed. Her every lick and nibble made him hiss.

Jack grabbed a handful of her hair and tugged her head back. "Behave. My way. Or no way. Understand?"

"Bossy."

"Yep." He cupped the outer swell of her stomach and started a trail of kisses from her sternum, straight down her belly. Rubbing his razor-stubbled cheek across the roundness until she squirmed. "But you are so fucking sexy when you're pregnant."

Also by
LORELEI JAMES

BLACKTOP COWBOYS® SERIES

Corralled

Saddled and Spurred

Wrangled and Tangled

One Night Rodeo

Turn and Burn

Hillbilly Rockstar

Wrapped and Strapped

Hang Tough

Racked and Stacked

Spun Out

BLACKTOP COWBOYS® NOVELLAS
1001 DARK NIGHTS

Roped In

Stripped Down

Strung Up

Tripped Out

Wound Tight

WILD WEST BOYS NOVELLAS

Mistress Christmas

Miss Firecracker

THE WANT YOU SERIES

I Want You Back

Want You to Want Me

THE NEED YOU SERIES

What You Need

Just What I Needed

All You Need

When I Need You

MASTERED SERIES

Bound

Unwound

Schooled (digital only novella)

Unraveled

Caged

STANDALONE NOVELS

Unbreak My Heart

Dirty Deeds

Running With The Devil

STANDALONE NOVELLAS

Lost In You

Wicked Garden

Ballroom Blitz

Printed in the USA
CPSIA information can be obtained
at www.ICGtesting.com
LVHW040427230823
756041LV00019B/203